W9-CIN-857

The Hat

The Hat

Holly Keller

Green Light Readers
Harcourt, Inc.

Orlando Austin New York San Diego Toronto London

Pam lost her hat.

Pam ran up.

Pam ran down.

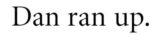

Dan ran up.

Dan ran down.

Dan got the hat!

Yay, Dan!
Yay, Pam!

Oh Where, Oh Where

Pam looked all over for her lost hat.

Sing "Oh Where, Oh Where Has My Little Dog Gone?" Use the word **hat** instead of **dog**.

as My Little Hat Gone?

where, oh where has my little hat gone?

where, oh where can it be?

th its brim so short and its ribbon so long,

where, oh where can it be?

Think About It

1. How does Pam lose her hat?

2. What does Pam do after she loses her hat?

3. How does Dan help Pam?

4. Would you want a friend like Dan? Why or why not?

5. What do you think Pam and Dan will do next?

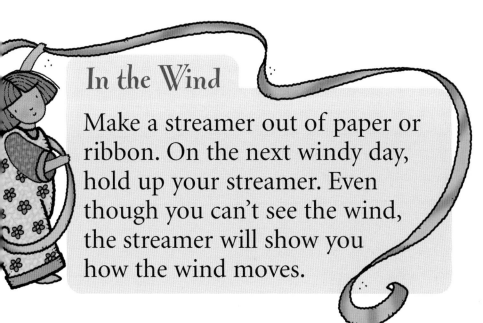

In the Wind

Make a streamer out of paper or ribbon. On the next windy day, hold up your streamer. Even though you can't see the wind, the streamer will show you how the wind moves.

Make a Hat

Use colored paper to make your own hat. Then make one for a friend. See if your hats will stay on when you're outside!

Meet the Author-Illustrator

In *The Hat*, Pam and Dan have quite an adventure when Pam's hat blows off. Holly Keller likes to write about friends and their adventures. She says, "It was great fun showing how Dan helps Pam. Good friends always help one another."

Holly Keller

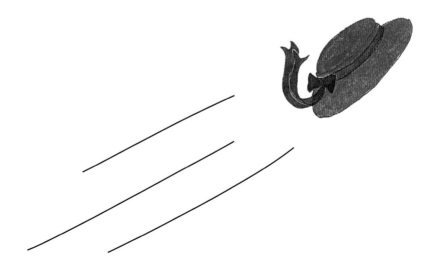

Copyright © 2003, 2001 by Harcourt, Inc.

All rights reserved. No part of this publication may be reproduced or transmitted
in any form or by any means, electronic or mechanical, including photocopy,
recording, or any information storage and retrieval system, without permission
in writing from the publisher.

For information about permission to reproduce selections from this book, write to trade.
permissions@hmhco.com or to Permissions, Houghton Mifflin Harcourt Publishing
Company, 3 Park Avenue, 19th Floor, New York, New York 10016.

www.hmhco.com

First Green Light Readers edition 2005
Green Light Readers is a trademark of Harcourt, Inc., registered in the
United States of America and/or other jurisdictions.

Library of Congress Cataloging-in-Publication Data
Keller, Holly.
The hat/Holly Keller.
p. cm.
"Green Light Readers."
Summary: Simple text tells how Dan helps Pam find her lost hat.
[1. Lost and found possessions—Fiction. 2. Hats—Fiction.] I. Title. II. Series:
Green Light reader.
PZ7.K28132Hat   2005
[E]—dc22   2004005823
ISBN 0-15-205179-1
ISBN 0-15-205178-3 pb

SCP 15 14 13
4500652194

Ages 4–6
Grade: K–1
Guided Reading Level: B
Reading Recovery Level: 3

Green Light Readers
For the reader who's ready to GO!

"A must-have for any family with a beginning reader."—*Boston Sunday Herald*

"You can't go wrong with adding several copies of these terrific books to your beginning-to-read collection."—*School Library Journal*

"A winner for the beginner."—*Booklist*

Five Tips to Help Your Child Become a Great Reader

1. Get involved. Reading aloud to and with your child is just as important as encouraging your child to read independently.

2. Be curious. Ask questions about what your child is reading.

3. Make reading fun. Allow your child to pick books on subjects that interest her or him.

4. Words are everywhere—not just in books. Practice reading signs, packages, and cereal boxes with your child.

5. Set a good example. Make sure your child sees YOU reading.

Why Green Light Readers Is the Best Series for Your New Reader

- Created exclusively for beginning readers by some of the biggest and brightest names in children's books

- Reinforces the reading skills your child is learning in school

- Encourages children to read—and finish—books by themselves

- Offers extra enrichment through fun, age-appropriate activities unique to each story

- Incorporates characteristics of the Reading Recovery program used by educators

- Developed with Harcourt School Publishers and credentialed educational consultants